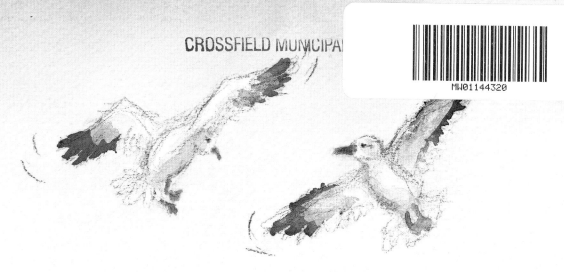

Copyright © 2005 by NordSüd Verlag AG, Gossau Zürich, Switzerland
First published in Switzerland under the title *Amoureux!*
English translation copyright © 2005 by North-South Books Inc., New York

First published in the United States, Great Britain, Canada, Australia, and New Zealand in 2005
by North-South Books, an imprint of NordSüd Verlag AG, Gossau Zürich, Switzerland.
Distributed in the United States by North-South Books Inc., New York.

Library of Congress Cataloging-in-Publication Data is available.
A CIP catalogue record for this book is available from The British Library.
ISBN 0-7358-2033-3 (trade edition)
10 9 8 7 6 5 4 3 2 1
Printed in Belgium

Udo Weigelt

Spring Fever

Illustrated by Sarah Emmanuelle Burg

Translated by Marianne Martens

North-South Books · New York · London

Spring was finally here! And with the warmer weather came freedom for Freddy, who had been cooped up inside all winter long.

As he padded along the street he saw that Mew was outside, too, relaxing on her windowsill, enjoying the spring sunshine. When she said hello, Freddy found himself admiring her eyes. She really does have especially pretty eyes, he thought.

But a minute later, Freddy was back on the prowl. "Ah ha!" he cried. "There's that mole that I almost caught last year." Freddy pounced and scooped up the mole in a flash. "All right, my good fellow," he said, "no more tunneling for you."

"Oh who cares," said the mole with a sigh. "I can't be bothered to dig and tunnel. Do you see that pretty mole over there? I just have to meet her."

"Excuse me?" said Freddy indignantly. "You should be quaking with fear. Don't you know that I am Freddy the Cat, and that your final hour has just arrived?"

"Oh, whatever," said the mole. "I just can't get her out of my head . . ."

Freddy was so shocked that he let the mole slip right through his claws. That mole is crazy, he thought. It's a good thing I didn't eat him—his craziness might be catching, like a cold.

Freddy continued on his way and just a moment later he spotted a sparrow and a hedgehog having a tug-of-war over a worm. In a flash, Freddy caught the sparrow, pinning it down with his paw.

"Ha! Ha! Guess your time is up," he said. "No more twittering for you."

"Oh twittering, schmittering, who cares," said the sparrow. "Do you see that bird over there on the fence? Isn't she just adorable?" The sparrow sighed deeply.

"Adorable? What are you talking about? It's just a sparrow," said Freddy.

"Just a sparrow?" shouted the sparrow. "That's not just a sparrow! She's THE sparrow!" He sighed again. "Antonia—the most beautiful sparrow far and wide. She's sweet and smart and beautiful and loving and totally adorable . . ."

"Would you stop it?" Freddy said, and let the sparrow go, although he wasn't really sure why.

"Has everyone gone completely crazy?" Freddy growled. "Why aren't they afraid of me?"

"They're all in love," mumbled the hedgehog.

"In love?" Freddy asked.

"Well of course they are. Haven't you noticed? They don't hear anything, they don't see anything—they only have eyes for their loved one. They're so in love they don't think straight, don't worry about danger. They're sure that when they're in love, nothing bad can happen to them. Haven't you ever been in love?"

"Me? No," Freddy replied.

"Too bad for you," said the hedgehog.

"Well, I mean I don't *think* I've ever been in love," Freddy said doubtfully. "Should I be?"

"Oh yes, it's the best thing in the world," said the hedgehog. "It's so exciting. Your heart pounds, you ache to be with your love, and when you are, it makes you unbelievably happy. You act silly and have fun together. It's just the best thing ever!"

"Did you say fun?" Freddy asked suspiciously.

"Yes, fun!" said the hedgehog. "Between you and me, I'm in love too . . ." He sighed happily.

In love, thought Freddy. Hmmm . . . Perhaps I should try it since everyone thinks it's such a great thing.

Freddy headed off down the street. As he turned the corner he spotted Mimi. She is quite beautiful, thought Freddy. A little bit vain, perhaps, but nice enough I suppose.

"Hello, Mimi," Freddy said politely.

"Hello, Freddy," said Mimi. She seemed a bit distracted. "Have you seen Sebastian?"

"No, I haven't seen that big tomcat for ages," Freddy replied. "Do you want to go chase some mice with me?"

"Chase mice? *Please! How gross*," said Mimi. "My paws will get all dirty. I think I'll look for Sebastian instead. Where could he be?"

"Who cares about Sebastian?" Freddy grumbled. Then he knew—Mimi does! She's in love with him, he thought. Well, I can't do anything about that.

Down on the beach Freddy met up with Tanya and Marlee. Tanya
was asking about Sebastian too, so Freddy studied Marlee for a bit.
She's okay, he thought, but . . .
Then he had a brainstorm. "Got to run," he cried. "See you later."

Freddy's heart was pounding and he felt happy and excited and a little bit anxious, too. Would she still be on her windowsill? he wondered.

She was!

"Hi there, Freddy," purred Mew. "I was hoping you'd be back."

She licked her paw tenderly and Freddy sighed deeply. He cleared his throat, then nervously asked, "Would you like to chase some mice with me?"

"I'd *love* to!" Mew purred.

And, tails together, off they went.